ONE MONDAY MORNING

ONE MONDAY MORNING

By Uri Shulevitz

Macmillan/McGraw-Hill School Publishing Company
New York Chicago Columbus

For information regarding permission, write to Charles Scribner's Sons, 866 Third Avenue, New York, NY 10022.

This edition is reprinted by arrangement with Charles Scribner's Sons, an imprint of Macmillan Publishing Company.

1995 Printing

Macmillan/McGraw-Hill School Division
10 Union Square East
New York, New York 10003

Printed in the United States of America

ISBN 0-02-179094-9 / 1, L. 1

6 7 8 9 FED 99 98 97 96 95 94

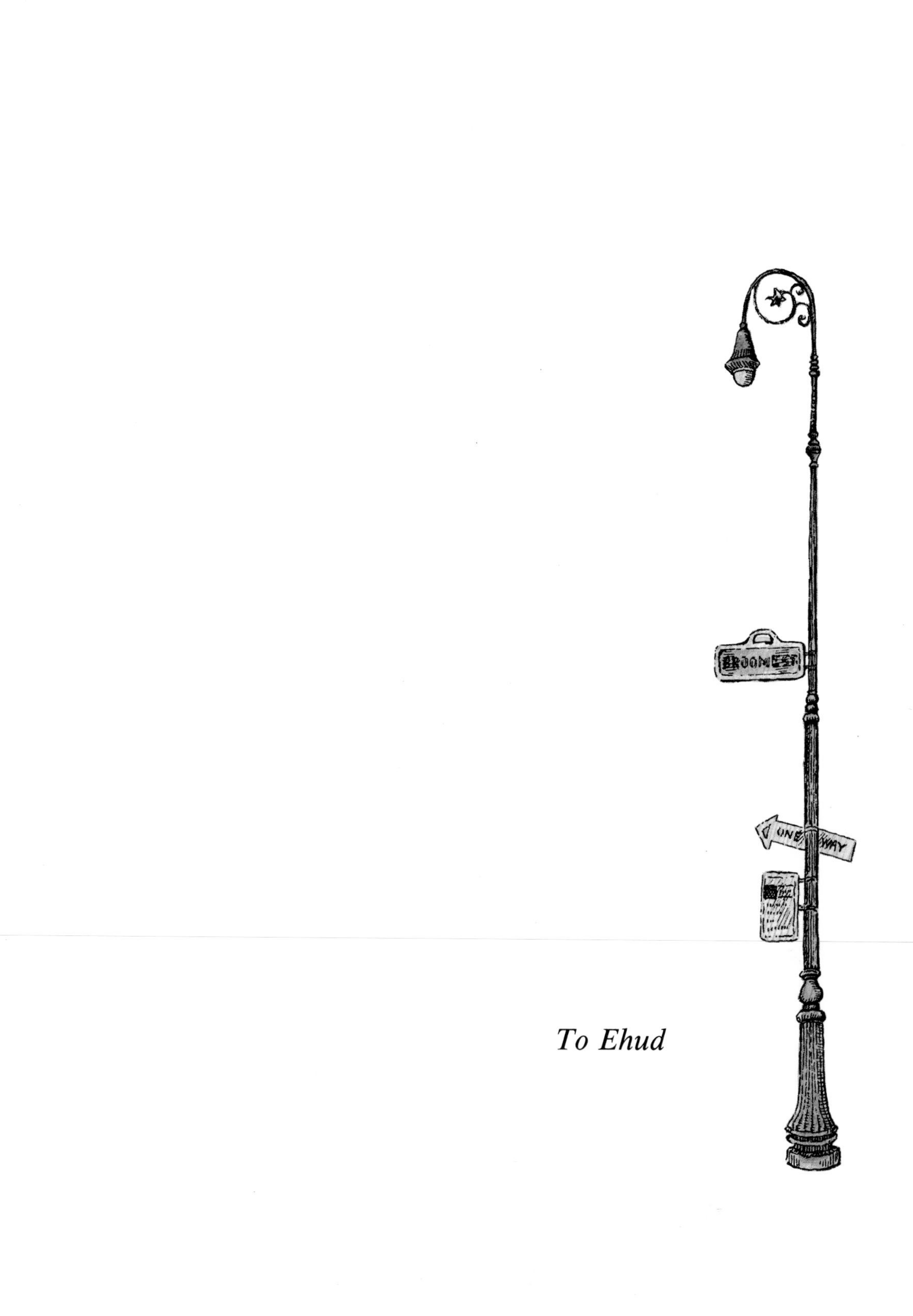

To Ehud

DWICHES
Cafe

One Monday morning

the king,

the queen, and the little prince came to visit me.

But I wasn't home.

So the little prince said,
"In that case we shall return on Tuesday."

On Tuesday morning the king, the queen, the little prince,

and the knight came to visit me.

But I wasn't home.

So the little prince said,
"In that case we shall return on Wednesday."

On Wednesday morning
the king,
the queen,
the little prince,
the knight,
and a royal guard
came to visit me.

But I wasn't home.

So the little prince said,
"In that case we shall return on Thursday."

On Thursday morning
the king, the queen,
the little prince,
the knight, a royal guard,
and the royal cook
came to visit me.

But I wasn't home.

So the little prince said,
"In that case we shall return on Friday."

3
LOOR

On Friday morning
the king, the queen,
the little prince,
the knight, a royal guard,
the royal cook,
and the royal barber
came to visit me.

But I wasn't home.

So the little prince said,
"In that case we shall return on Saturday."

5
FLOOR

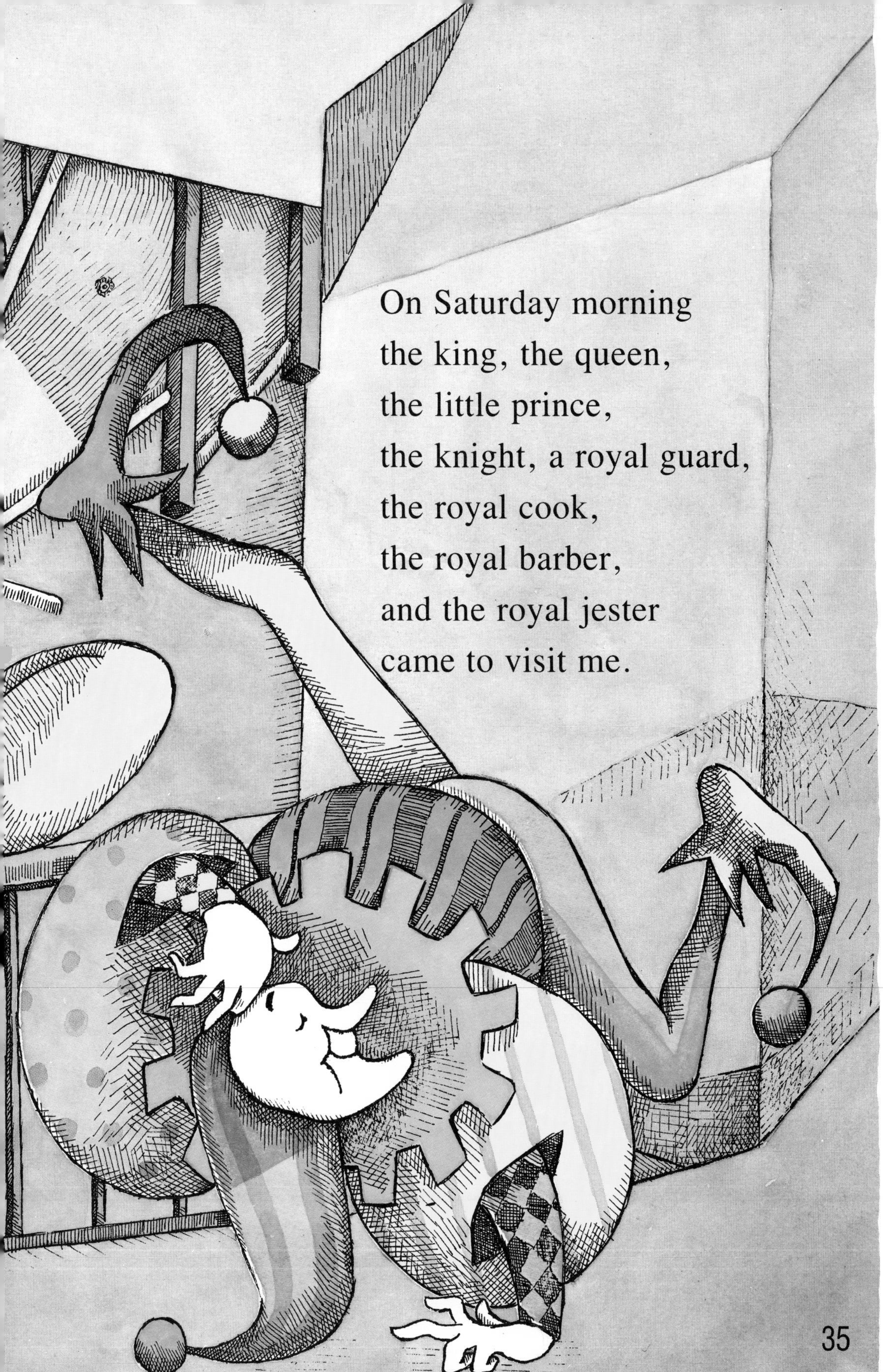

On Saturday morning
the king, the queen,
the little prince,
the knight, a royal guard,
the royal cook,
the royal barber,
and the royal jester
came to visit me.

But I wasn't home.

So the little prince said,
"In that case we shall return on Sunday."

6
FLOOR

On Sunday morning the king, the queen,
the little prince, the knight,
a royal guard,

the royal cook,
the royal barber,
the royal jester,
and a little dog
came to visit me.

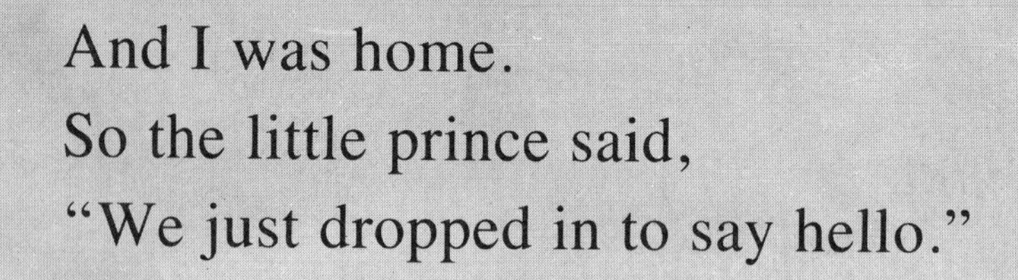

And I was home.
So the little prince said,
"We just dropped in to say hello."

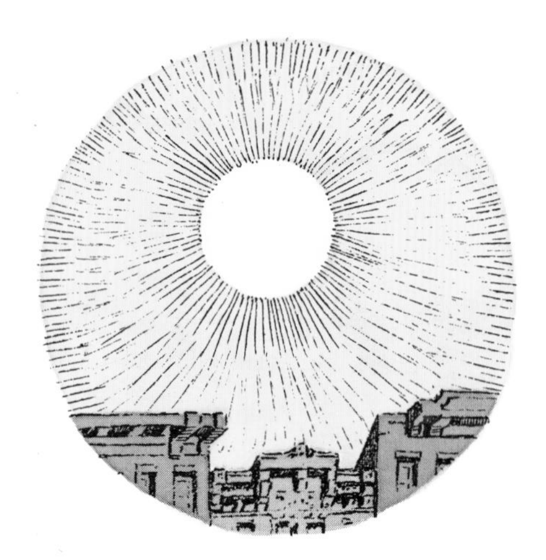